Grandma, Granddad, We Want to Praise God

Written by
Vanessa Fortenberry

Illustrated by Sharon Grey

BQB

North Carolina

Published in the United States by BQB Publishing
(an imprint of Boutique of Quality Books Publishing Company)
www.bqbpublishing.com

Printed in the United States of America

978-1-952782-21-3 (h)
978-1-952782-22-0 (e)

Library of Congress Control Number: 2021942275

Editor: Andrea Vande Vorde
Book design: Robin Krauss, www.bookformatters.com
Cover and interior illustrations: Sharon Grey, www.sharongreywatercolors.com

For information about special discounts for bulk purchases, please contact BQB Special Sales at Terri@bqbpublishing.com

Train up a child in the way he should go: and when he is old,
he will not depart from it.
— *Proverbs 22:6 (KJV)*

———————

The dedication of this book belongs to my Heavenly Father;
the "Bread of Life," the "Light of the World," the "Lily of the Valley,"
and the "Lamb of God!"

———————

This story breathes life because of my parents and my grandmother, who taught me as a young child to praise God.

A special shout out to grandparents around the world who exhibit God's love and who support their grandchildren in their quest to see God, to know Him, and to praise Him.

Special thanks to my mentor, Crystal Bowman for her editorial help and keen insight in preparing my manuscript; my publisher and project manager, Terri Leidich, who has supported my vision for writing God's Word; my editor, Andrea Vande Vorde, who allowed me to maintain my author's voice and style; my amazing and gifted illustrator, Sharon Grey, who captured my words and brought them to life; and my book designer, Robin Krauss, who creates visual grace to complement the text and illustrations.

Finally, but not least, I thank my family, friends, and reading fans. You are my cheerleaders who have continued to support and encourage me throughout my writing journey.

Love and blessings to all,
Vanessa Fortenberry

I will praise the Lord at all times,
His praise is always on my lips.

— *Psalm 34:1 (NCV)*

"Grandma, Granddad, we want to praise God.
I wonder...what does praising God mean?"
Grandma clapped, "Praise shows our thanks,
to a loving God who is not seen."

"Granddad, we want to praise God. How do we praise a God we can't see?"
"When we accept God as our friend, we see Jesus who's in you and me."

"Grandma, we want to praise God.
Why should we give Him praise?"
"Thank God for His goodness and love.
God made you! Respect Him all your days."

"Granddad, we want to praise God. Should we praise God for Jesus?" He smiled. "Honor God for His Son; He died and gave His life for us."

7

"Granddad, we want to praise God.
Why should we bless His name?"
"When we lift up the name of God,
our lives change; we can't stay the same."

"Grandma, we want to praise God.
What is the best time to praise Him?"
She danced. "Praise God throughout the day.
He's worthy; don't let your praise dim."

"Granddad, we want to praise God. Do we thank Him when things go wrong?" Granddad smiled. "Child, life is not easy, but, it's good. That's why I sing my song."

"Grandma, we want to praise God. But we don't know how to start."
"Pray and have a little talk with God. Listen to Him with an open heart."

"Praise God with your thoughts and your words. Allow the light in you to shine. God gives us this light for us to keep. Glow for Jesus; it's yours and it's mine."

"Praise God anytime and anywhere. He loved you first, now you show your love. Praise Him with others and by yourself. Give glory to the one above."

14

"We got it! And, now we understand. We'll praise God whether happy or sad. We will praise Him from morning 'til night. We'll take it from here, Grandma and Granddad."

"Let us lift our hands, sing, clap and dance—
At a game, at school, and at God's house.
We can thank God in so
many ways. We can
roar like a lion or be
quiet as a mouse."

"It's okay when we feel sad and blue,
We'll keep praising God anyway.
God gives us strength when we struggle.
So, we hold onto our faith and pray."

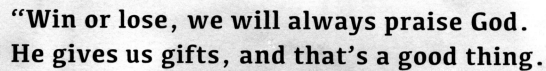

"Win or lose, we will always praise God.
He gives us gifts, and that's a good thing.
Even small thoughts can make big
changes. Believe...and see what
His love will bring."

"Dinner is served and on the table.
Let's thank God for our food today.
God is good. He makes sure we are
fed. Let's sit down, bow our heads,
and pray."

"Let's honor God for our parents, grandparents, and caretakers who led us all to love, worship, and praise Him— It's all there in the Bible we read."

"Why praise God?" Grandma and Granddad asked.

"Cause if we don't, the rocks will cry out.
God made us to praise Him only.
We can't hold it in . . . that's why we
shout!"

They asked Jesus, "Do you hear what these children are saying?"
"Yes," Jesus replied. "Haven't you ever read the Scriptures? For they say, 'You have taught children and infants to give You praise.'"

— Matthew 21:16 (NLT)

Families Growing in Faith

Enjoy other books in the series:
Families Growing in Faith.

Mama, I Want to See God

Written by
Vanessa Fortenberry

Illustrated by Leah Jennings

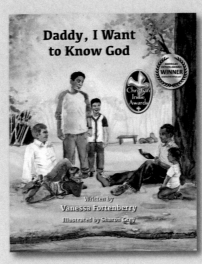

Daddy, I Want to Know God

Written by
Vanessa Fortenberry

Illustrated by Sharon Grey

Grandma, Granddad, We Want to Praise God

Written by
Vanessa Fortenberry

Illustrated by Sharon Grey

Available in Print, eBook, and Audio.

A Special Request:
Please take a moment to leave a review (comment) for these books
at your favorite book retailer.

Your support is appreciated!